Neptune

the Magic Sea Pony

For Gerard, with love – SK
To Adrienne, Alex and Tom – ST

SIMON AND SCHUSTER

First published in Great Britain in 2009 by Simon and Schuster UK Ltd

1st Floor, 222 Gray's Inn Road, London WC1X 8HB

A CBS Company

A CIP catalogue record for this book is available from the British Library upon request

ISBN: 978 1 84738 533 8

Printed in China

5 7 9 10 8 6 4

Princess Evie's Ponies

Neptune the Magic Sea Pony

Sarah KilBride

Illustrated by Sophie Tilley

SIMON AND SCHUSTER

London   New York   Sydney

At Starlight Stables, Princess Evie was busy grooming her ponies. Her kitten, Sparkles, watched as she led them out of their stables one by one.

"Where shall we go today?" Evie whispered as she combed their glossy manes.

You see, Evie's ponies weren't just any old ponies.

They were magic ponies!

Whenever Evie rode them, she was whisked away
on a magical adventure in a faraway land.

"Neptune," said Evie. "Let's go!"

Neptune was a dappled grey pony with blue eyes and
a silver mane.

Princess Evie saddled her up. Then she put on her rucksack
full of useful things. Sparkles hopped up onto Evie's
shoulder ready for adventure.

Off they galloped faster and faster,

through the tunnel of trees.

Evie closed her eyes.

Where would the tunnel take them today?

With a neigh, Neptune charged out of the tunnel. Evie opened
her eyes. They were galloping along a beach of golden sand!
Evie's dress was all the colours of the ocean and it sparkled
like the waves.

Neptune's mane shimmered with silver and the softest sea blue.
Her bridle was decorated with the prettiest seashells, and
droplets of seawater on her reins glittered like diamonds.
Up ahead, Evie spotted a figure sitting on the rocks.

It was a mermaid!

"Hello," said Evie. "I'm Evie.
This is my pony, Neptune,
and this is my kitten, Sparkles."
The mermaid turned around.
Her eyes were full of tears.

"I'm Periwinkle," she sniffed. "Please, will you and your sea pony help me? I've lost my precious pink pearl and I need it for the Mermaid Queen's Parade."

"Wow!" thought Evie. "Neptune – a sea pony!"

Of course they would help!

In a flash, Periwinkle was on Neptune's back and soon they were galloping faster and faster . . .

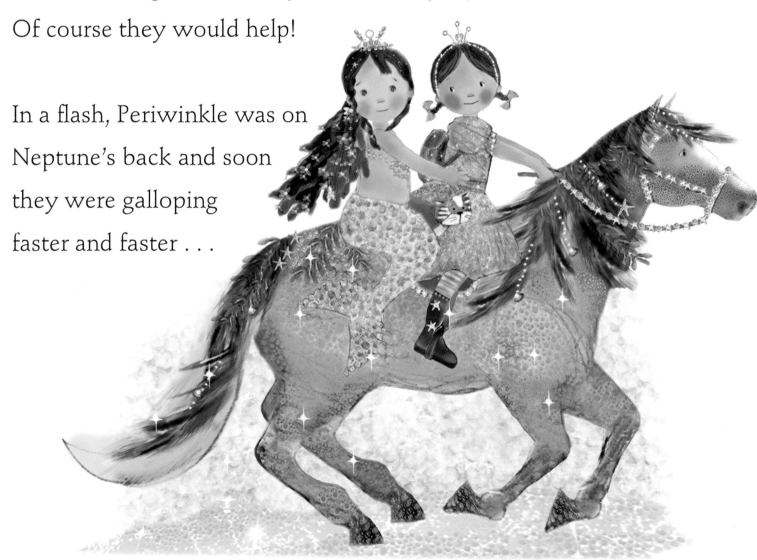

... until, suddenly, they were on the sea bed,
deep below the waves.

"Have you seen a precious pink pearl?" Evie asked some
spiky sea urchins.

"Yes, we've seen it," they said. "It came bobbing along on
the tide. We smoothed and polished it with our sponges
but then it bobbed away."

"Oh, no!" sighed Periwinkle. "Now I'll never find it!"

But Neptune wasn't going to give up that easily.

Together they all swam deeper and deeper, and spotted an octopus. "Madam O!" called Periwinkle. "Have you seen my precious pink pearl? It fell off my crown when I was polishing it in a rock pool."

"Yes, I've seen it," replied Madam O. "I was practising my juggling when your pearl came floating by. I tried to juggle with it but I got in a tangle and it floated off towards that cave."

They all rushed towards
the deep sea cave. The Mermaid
Queen's Parade would be starting
soon. Could they find the pearl in time?
Neptune and Periwinkle looked inside
clam shells and under seaweed.
Princess Evie searched around
the starfish and in between
barnacles. Sparkles even
looked under a crab!

But the pearl was nowhere to be seen.

"It's no use," said Periwinkle, blinking back tears.
"We'll never find it."

Just then, Sparkles' ears pricked up.
There was a loud whooping
and cheering.

"Look!" pointed Evie. "The dolphins are playing football!"

"That's not football, it's flipball," laughed Periwinkle.

"And that's not a ball – it's my pink pearl!"

"Excuse us," said Evie. "Could we please have that pink pearl back? Periwinkle needs it for the Mermaid Queen's Parade."

The captain shook his head.

"Sorry, ladies. We've been waiting for the tide to bring us a ball for ages. You'll have to wait until the flipball championships are over."

"What am I going to do?" sighed Periwinkle.
"I need my pearl now."
Evie had an idea!
She searched through her rucksack
of useful things. She found a hanky
and a magnet. Then Sparkles
pulled out some string and
a marble!

"Well done, Sparkles," Evie smiled. "That's just the thing!"
She swam up to the captain and threw the marble in
the air. "Let's swap."

Periwinkle collected the pink pearl and carefully placed it
in her crown.

Now they just had to get to the parade!
Neptune galloped faster than ever before.

They arrived at the sea palace just in time!
What a magical sight! Periwinkle took her place alongside the other mermaids and carried the Queen's cloak. Princess Evie and Neptune proudly led the sea horses, and Sparkles helped the butterfly fish to carry the banners.

The sea urchins cheered and the dolphins squeaked. Shoals of angelfish glistened all around, and everyone sang along to the sound of the trumpet fish playing their ocean tunes.

After the parade, it was time for Princess Evie, Neptune and Sparkles to go home. Periwinkle gave them each a big hug.

"Thank you for helping me," she said. "I'll never forget!"
"Neither will I!" said Evie.

She waved back at Periwinkle, as Neptune cantered along the sea bed, then across the golden beach and through the tunnel of trees.

Back at Starlight Stables, Neptune let out a neigh and shook her mane. Some seaweed fell to the ground – and so did something shiny. Sparkles caught it with his paw. It was a tiny purse! Inside was a silver bracelet with a precious pink pearl. Periwinkle must have tied it to Neptune's bridle.

"Thank you, Periwinkle," whispered Princess Evie. "And thank you, Neptune," she said, stroking her pony's mane. "You saved the day. What a VERY special sea pony!"

"Miaow!" agreed Sparkles.